THE BLACK KNIGHT
of
GRESSINGHAM

THE BLACK KNIGHT
of
GRESSINGHAM

Philip Ardagh

With illustrations by
Mike Phillips

Barrington Stoke

First published in 2015 in Great Britain by
Barrington Stoke Ltd
18 Walker Street, Edinburgh, EH3 7LP

www.barringtonstoke.co.uk

Text © 2015 Philip Ardagh
Illustrations © 2015 Mike Phillips

The moral right of Philip Ardagh and Mike Phillips to be
identified as the author and illustrator of this work has
been asserted in accordance with the Copyright, Designs
and Patents Act, 1988

A CIP catalogue record for this book is available
from the British Library upon request

ISBN: 978-1-78112-407-9

Printed in China by Leo

CONTENTS

There are many tales about the Green Men of Gressingham, the famous outlaws of Gressingham Forest. Tales about their fight for what is right and about their brave deeds. Tales about their clever tricks and their brown clothes. (They liked brown because it hid the dirt better than green and they blended in with the trees.)

You may have heard about how they defeated the evil Marshal Guppy or how they went in search of dragons. But you won't have heard the tale of the Black Knight, unless you have read this book before!

Our story begins with a bang on a door ...

Chapter 1
Bang! Bang!

The bangs on the cottage door were getting louder and louder. In fact, it wasn't really a cottage. It was more of a hovel. And it wasn't really a door. It was more of a number of odd-shaped planks that had been nailed together by someone who wasn't very good at nailing things.

The person who wasn't very good at nailing things was a very small man named Squat. Right now, Squat was in bed, where he was doing his very best to ignore the bangs on the door. Poor people didn't have proper beds in those days. Squat's bed was a pile of straw, and he had an old flour sack as a blanket. The sack covered most of him because he was so small.

Squat pulled the sack over his head as the bangs got louder. When the bangs got even louder still, he tried sticking some of the straw from his bed in his ears. It prickled. Squat gave up and got up to open the door. There was no need.

With one last, loud BANG the door gave way at last. It fell flat on the hard mud floor of Squat's hovel. It only just missed Squat, who jumped to one side.

"Sorry!" a loud voice boomed. In came a man so tall that he seemed to take up the whole hovel.

"Big Jim!" Squat gasped. He looked at his old friend, who was dressed in the brown clothes of an outlaw. "What are you doing here?" he asked.

Big Jim lifted up the door and tried to fix it back in place. "I'm here because we need your help," he said.

Big Jim needed Squat's help? How on earth could Squat help Jim?

"Pull up a stool and sit down," Squat said. There was only one stool but Squat hoped that Big Jim would take up less room sitting down.

So Big Jim sat on the stool. His knees almost came up to his nose. He made Squat think of the frog in the pond behind the hovel.

"We need you!" Big Jim said. "We want you to join."

"Join what?" Squat asked. Squat was hoping Big Jim was going to ask him to join two planks of wood together, or two pieces of string.

"Join the Green Men of Gressingham!" Big Jim said. "Join us and become an outlaw!"

Squat had been afraid that Jim was going to say that. He was not sure that he was brave enough to be an outlaw. The outlaws loved a good fight.

"Why?" he asked with a gulp. "I can't fire a bow and arrow and I don't know how to fight with a sword or with my fists."

Big Jim looked at his friend. Big Jim made most people look small, but Squat really was tiny. Big Jim towered over him even now, when he was sitting down and Squat was standing up.

"We have a special mission and we all agreed that you are the only man for the job," Big Jim said.

"You did?" Squat said. His face went red. This was because he was glowing with pride. Squat didn't often glow with pride. In fact, he had never glowed with pride before. It felt good.

"All of you agreed?" Squat asked. "All of the Green Men?" (He wanted to hear Big Jim say it again.)

"Yes," Big Jim said. "Even Robyn-in-the-Hat agreed."

Squat glowed with even more pride. Robyn-in-the-Hat was the most famous person for miles around. People sang songs about her, around fires on dark nights. They told tales and whispered rumours of her brave deeds.

Robyn-in-the-Hat was the leader of the Green Men of Gressingham, but she wasn't a poor peasant or a monk like her men. She was a rich lady with sparkling blue eyes. But her face was hidden by a strange mask fixed to her hat. She was a living, breathing MYSTERY. (There. I wrote the word in capital letters to show just what a big mystery she was.)

"And what is this special mission you need me for?" Squat asked. He was very proud now.

"I can't tell you," Big Jim said. "I can't tell you unless you agree to become one of the Green Men first!"

"Can I have time to think?" Squat asked. If he became a Green Man, he would have to leave his old life behind. He would have to leave this hovel that he called home, and the friendly frog.

But time was one thing Squat did not have.

Chapter 2
The Enemy

Big Jim was about to say something when he heard a noise outside.

It was the sound of horses' hooves on hard earth and the chinking of soldiers' chain-mail.

Then a voice called out. "Come out, in the name of Lord Dashwood, peasant!"

Squat was happy to admit that he was a peasant. He was born a peasant and he was pretty sure that he would die a peasant. But he didn't like the way the voice outside his hovel had said the word 'peasant'. It had said it as if Squat were a worthless piece of nothing.

But Squat wasn't a worthless piece of nothing. He was a human being with feelings. And, just because he was very small, it did not mean his feelings weren't every bit as big as everyone else's.

Squat opened his sort-of door that Big Jim had sort-of fixed and blinked in the morning light. He found himself face to face with none other than Marshal Guppy. Yes, it was the evil Marshal Guppy, the man who ruled the local lands for Lord Dashwood of Dashwood Castle.

The Marshal was on a big grey horse and two foot soldiers stood on each side. The four soldiers looked a little red in the face from running to keep up with the horse. And they also looked a little cross. It wasn't fair. They were the ones with heavy chain-mail and heavy

swords, but Marshall Guppy was the one on the horse!

Marshal Guppy raised an eyebrow. "Aha!" he said. "I was wrong. There is not one peasant here but two. And in such a tiny ..." He stared at Squat's hovel as if he couldn't think of a word to describe it. "... A tiny space," he said at last. "Come on out, Big Jim. I know you are in there!"

Big Jim ducked out the small door to face his enemy.

"What have we here, little man?" Guppy said to Squat. "You dare to hide an outlaw in your home?"

Before Big Jim or Squat had a chance to say anything, the Marshal nodded at the four soldiers. They drew their big, flat swords.

"ARREST THEM!" Marshal Guppy commanded.

Two of the soldiers strode over to Big Jim.

The other two strode over to Squat.

This was a big mistake.

All four of them should have gone for Big Jim.

Big Jim picked up the two soldiers nearest to him – one in each hand. He banged their heads together with a loud CLANG. Their helmets fell to the ground and rolled around on the grass. Then their swords fell from their hands and they groaned and toppled to the ground.

If this story were a cartoon, the soldiers would have gone cross-eyed, stuck out their tongues, and little tweeting birds would have fluttered around their heads.

Squat snatched one of the swords from the ground. It was very heavy and almost as tall as he was, so he had to hold it in both hands. He waved it around in front of him. The two soldiers that were left looked nervous.

While this was happening, Big Jim picked up the other sword, spun it over his head and let it fly. He wasn't aiming at the soldiers – he was aiming at Marshal Guppy. The Marshal's eyes opened wide in horror and surprise. He pulled on his horse's reins, jabbed its sides with his spurs and galloped off as fast as he could. The sword only just missed him.

The two soldiers turned and ran.

"Nice work, Squat," Big Jim said. He slapped Squat on the back as they watched the soldiers go.

A slap on the back from Big Jim was a bit like being kicked by Nancy, Max the Miller's donkey. The slap made Squat drop his sword, but he managed not to fall flat on his face.

Squat grinned. It wasn't every day that someone gave Marshal Guppy a taste of his own medicine.

"What do we do now?" he asked.

"We tie up these two," Big Jim said. He dragged the two soldiers to a tree. "Give me a hand, will you?"

They sat one soldier up on one side of the tree trunk and the other soldier on the other. Squat fetched a rope and they tied it around the men.

"Now there's no way you can stay here," Big Jim told Squat. "You've stood up to Marshal Guppy. You are a wanted man!"

"So now I am an outlaw if I like it or not!" Squat said.

"Yes," Big Jim said. He bent down and shook Squat's hand. "Welcome to the Green Men of Gressingham."

Chapter 3
Friend or Foe?

It took a while for Squat and Big Jim to reach
the Green Men's secret camp. It was hidden
deep in Gressingham Forest.

In modern times, there are two main uses
for forests.

1. to grow trees for timber and paper.

2. to have places where you can have nice
walks and point at things and say, "Ooo! Look
at that bird!" or "That's a pretty leaf!"

Back in the days of the Green Men, powerful families lived in castles and ruled their lands the way the kings ruled their countries. And lots of those lands were covered by forests. Those forests were very busy places. People found food there for themselves and their animals – mushrooms and berries and sweet chestnuts. Pigs snuffled about for tasty acorns. Folk collected fire wood. They burned charcoal. They cut twigs from willow trees to weave into baskets and chairs. And the rich hunted stags and wild boar.

So the Green Men's secret camp needed to be somewhere off the beaten track. It was near a stream, but not so close as to be soggy. And it had an excellent look-out tree.

As Big Jim and Squat arrived, two Green Men slid out of the tree and landed in front of them. They were called Fidget and Friendly and they hit the ground at the same time with one big THUMP!

"You came!" Fidget said.

"I didn't have much choice!" Squat said,
with a grin almost as big as his face. He'd been
friends with Fidget before Fidget had joined the
Green Men. They used to work together in Lord
Dashwood's fields.

"Did you have to twist his arm?" Friendly asked Big Jim.

"Marshal Guppy helped you make up your mind, didn't he, Squat?" Big Jim said with a smile.

Friendly gave a friendly laugh. "That was nice of him. What happened?"

Big Jim and Squat told them what had happened as they walked into the camp.

In the middle of the camp, a bubbling cauldron of soup was cooking over an open fire. A man called Physic was stirring it.

Physic was a plump monk. He had a strange haircut and a monk's tunic, which is called a habit. His habit was made from the same brown material as all the other Green Men's outfits.

Next to Physic, Squat saw none other than Robyn-in-the-Hat herself.

All of a sudden Squat felt all nervous and shy. Robyn was not only a Gressingham legend but also a real lady.

But Squat didn't stay nervous for long. Robyn threw her arms around him and lifted him off his feet. His legs kicked in the air. "Thank you for joining us, brave Squat!" she said. She kissed him on the top of his head and put him back down again. "Now, we have business to discuss," she said.

Squat could not believe how fast his life had changed. When he went to bed the night before he had been a peasant. But when morning came, he'd turned into an outlaw!

"Gather the men, Jim," Robyn-in-the-Hat said. Soon everyone was sitting in the clearing in the middle of the camp, except for two look-outs.

"As most of you know," Robyn said, "Marshal Guppy has a new weapon in his war against good. This weapon is a man. He is a knight. He

24

is French. He is Sir Jack de Zack. He will fight
for any reason in return for gold. And Marshal
Guppy pays him very well indeed."

"I saw Sir Jack at a jousting match last
month," Big Jim said. "He knocked another

knight off his horse, then he hacked him with his sword and beat him with his mace. He showed no mercy. He was a fighting machine!"

"I remember one time Sam the Shepherd was crossing the wooden bridge at Washford," Friendly said. "Sir Jack wanted to ride across the other way. He hacked at the sheep with his sword to clear his path."

There were boos and hisses from the Green Men. They did not like to hear about people being bad to animals. Friendly patted Martha the pig, who had come over to investigate the smell of soup.

"Things are bad enough for the people of Gressingham with all these new laws, taxes and rules from Dashwood Castle," Robyn said. "Now Marshal Guppy wants to scare them with this horrid knight. We must make sure that Sir Jack de Zack goes back to France and stays there. This is where you come in, Squat."

"Me?" Squat said. He was not sure he'd heard her right. "But how?"

"There are not many ways to stop a man like Sir Jack," Robyn said. "We could kill him –"

"But we do not believe in killing," Big Jim broke in.

"We could defeat him so that he is too ashamed to show his face around here again," Robyn said.

"But who can defeat such a powerful knight?" Big Jim said.

"Or we could scare him away," Robyn said.

"And that's where you get to play your part, Squat," Big Jim said with a grin.

Squat gasped. "Me? Scare away the meanest knight in the land? But how?"

Chapter 4
Revenge

Marshal Guppy was in a bad mood. He was in more than a bad mood. He was furious. He rode up to the moat of Dashwood Castle. He couldn't get across because the drawbridge was up.

"Let me enter!" he shouted.

"Who goes there?" a guard called down from the tower at the gate.

"Me!" Guppy screamed. "Let me in!"

The guard peered out. "Who's me –?" he began.

"IT'S MARSHAL GUPPY AND IF YOU DON'T PUT DOWN THE DRAWBRIDGE THIS INSTANT, I WILL THROW YOU INTO THE MOAT. THEN, IF YOU DON'T DROWN, I WILL THROW YOU INTO THE DEEPEST DUNGEON AND HANG YOU

UPSIDE-DOWN BY YOUR FEET FOR A YEAR AND A DAY ... DO I MAKE MYSELF CLEAR?"

"Yes, sire!" the guard said. He was used to the Marshal's rages, but he had never seen Marshal Guppy quite so red in the face before. The drawbridge came down.

As soon as the front of the drawbridge touched the ground, Marshal Guppy was across it. His horse's hooves made a loud clattering noise on the cobbles as he galloped into the courtyard.

"RAMBLE?" Guppy shouted, as he swung down to the ground.

"Yes, sire?" A tall, thin man stepped out of the shadows.

Guppy looked calmer. "Have Sir Jack de Zack meet me in my private rooms," he ordered.

"Right away, sire," Ramble said, with a nod.

Guppy ducked in a doorway and up a spiral staircase. He threw open the door of his rooms, marched inside and flung himself on his bed.

He couldn't stop thinking about Big Jim. "NO ONE MAKES A FOOL OUT OF GUPPY!" he shouted to himself.

The noise startled a dove that had been sleeping on the window ledge. The flap of its wings as it flew away made Guppy jump and feel rather foolish.

There was a knock at the door and in strode Sir Jack de Zack. He clanked as he walked because he was fully dressed in his gleaming silver armour.

"Do you even sleep in your armour?" Guppy mocked.

"I will if you pay me to," Sir Jack said in his French accent. "A good knight must always be ready for battle!"

"But you are a bad knight," Marshal Guppy said with an evil sneer.

"I think you mean a bad man, Marshal," said Sir Jack. "I do not fight for what is right but for who pays the most ... but I fight well. Perhaps that makes me a good bad knight!"

Now both men laughed in a rather nasty way.

"I saw Big Jim the outlaw near the village today," Marshal Guppy told Sir Jack. "Those Green Men are getting bolder and making more trouble every day. I want you to take as many men as you need to finish them off for good. Crush them. Stamp on them. SNUFF THEM OUT LIKE A CANDLE."

"That would be my pleasure, Marshal," Sir Jack de Zack said, with a bow.

"But don't harm their leader Robyn-in-the-Hat," the Marshal said. "I want her here as my prisoner. Then I can rip off her mask and reveal her true face."

"Very good, Marshal," Sir Jack said. "Or perhaps I mean very bad! I must go and make my plans." He turned and clanked back to the door.

"Do it tomorrow," Marshal Guppy said.

"Tomorrow?" Sir Jack said. He stopped in his tracks and the smile fell from his face. "*Non, non, non.* It is not possible."

"You need more time?" Marshal Guppy snapped.

"It is not that," Sir Jack said. "It is my Moon chart. There is a bad Moon tomorrow. I will not attack then."

Marshal Guppy shook his head. He knew that it was no good to argue with Sir Jack about bad omens. Sir Jack's room was full of Moon charts, star charts and good luck charms. This was the price Marshal Guppy had to pay to have such a demon fighter on his side.

"Very well," he said. "Hunt them down on Saturday instead."

Chapter 5
Plans

All the Green Men made their newest and smallest member welcome. They were pleased that Squat did not scream or run and hide when Robyn explained the plan to defeat Sir Jack and what Squat would have to do.

"It will be dangerous," Robyn said. "Will you do it?"

"Of course!" Squat said. He did not feel as brave as he sounded.

The other Green Men cheered.

"Would now be a good time for soup?"
Physic asked. He thought that any time was a
good time for food.

"An excellent time!" said Robyn-in-the-Hat.

There was another loud cheer and a clatter
of wooden soup bowls and spoons.

Robyn-in-the-Hat looked at Squat with her sparkling blue eyes. "You are a small man with a brave heart and a big part in our plan," she said. "Thank you, Squat. We must find you an outlaw's uniform as soon as we can. Now I must leave as I have duties in my other life. I will return at sundown."

Robyn jumped onto her horse and galloped off between the trees.

When they had eaten their soup, Big Jim led Squat over to the edge of the outlaws' camp. Here there was a rocky hill, dotted with scrubby plants and bushes.

"Up here!" Big Jim said. He leaped up the hill and waited by a large bush with sharp, pointy leaves.

Squat scrambled up after him. Jim pulled aside the bush and Squat saw the mouth of a cave. Jim ducked inside and Squat followed. Light from a hole high up in the rocky roof lit parts of the cave, but much of it was still in shadow.

"What an amazing place!" Squat said in wonder.

"Yes," said Big Jim. "If our enemies ever discover our camp, this cave will be our secret hiding place."

Just then the hairs on the back of Squat's neck began to prickle. He had the strange feeling that they were not alone. He spun around and looked into the shadows.

There was a glint of metal.

Squat peered deeper and gasped.

In the back of the cave Squat saw a huge knight in jet-black armour, gripping an enormous sword.

Chapter 6
In or Out?

The next morning was as sunny as the last. The birds were singing. But it was Friday and Sir Jack de Zack's charts had made it very clear that it would not be a good day.

"Should I stay indoors or go outside?" he asked the squire whose job was to look after him.

"It might be safer to stay indoors, sire," said the squire, who was used to his master's beliefs.

"But the roof may fall in and crush me or I may fall down the stairs and break my neck!" said Sir Jack.

"Then you might be safer outdoors," the squire agreed.

"But I may fall from my horse or be trampled by cows."

"Then indoors would be better," said the squire.

"But I may knock over a candle and trap myself in a sheet of flame!"

And so the debate went on, back and forth, back and forth for a good ten minutes.

You may have spotted that not one of Sir Jack de Zack's fears involved other people. He had no reason to be afraid of people. He would fight anyone. And he never lost a fight.

Sir Jack decided his best bet was to stay indoors and make plans for the next day's sport – the hunt for the Green Men of Gressingham.

And the next day came soon enough, as next days do.

Sir Jack clattered across the courtyard on his fine horse. The drawbridge was lowered and he cantered out of Dashwood Castle. A dozen other knights and a small army of foot soldiers met him there.

"Today we have one aim," Sir Jack announced. "We are going to rid Gressingham of those thieves and murderers who call themselves the Green Men. They have been a thorn in Lord Dashwood's side for too long. Only their leader Robyn-in-the-Hat must remain alive."

"Will there be no trial, Sir Jack?" one of the knights asked. "Should we not capture them and –?"

"Why waste time?" Sir Jack interrupted. "They would be hanged anyway. Come!"

The fastest way to reach the forest was to cross a stone bridge at a place called Stonebridge Crossing. Can you guess how it got its name?

When Sir Jack de Zack and his men reached the bridge, their way was blocked. A man sat on his horse in the very middle of the bridge. The horse was huge. It was the size of a carthorse used to pull heavy wagons. And the man? He looked huge too. He was covered from head to toe in black armour. He held a sword in his right hand. Its blade was not silver, but was as black as night.

"Let me pass, Black Knight, in the name of Lord Dashwood!" Sir Jack de Zack shouted. "We have rats to catch!"

"You shall not pass," the Black Knight boomed back.

"Is that a threat?" Sir Jack asked. His mouth curled into a sneer.

"It is a promise," said the Black Knight.

Chapter 7
Challenge

Now Sir Jack de Zack was a happy man. He had the chance to fight a fellow knight. He would enjoy defeating this man in black.

"You think you can stop us crossing that bridge?" Sir Jack shouted. "My soldiers could hack you down in an instant."

"They could, sir," the Black Knight boomed. "But I challenge you to fight me, man to man."

"Just you and I?" said Sir Jack.

"Just you and I," the Black Knight said, and his helmet nodded. "And if I win, your men will turn back to Dashwood Castle."

"Very well," Sir Jack said. "But you will not win." He turned to face his men. "You heard the challenge." He laughed. "If this Black Knight wins, then you all return to the castle."

Before the final words had left his mouth, Sir Jack was galloping onto the bridge. He had his sword ready in his hand.

The Black Knight did not move. He sat in his saddle as if he didn't have a care in the world.

Sir Jack charged up the arch of the bridge, right into the middle where the Black Knight sat. He roared like a wild animal and crashed his sword down on his enemy.

CLANG!

The Black Knight's head came off his body with a single slash of Sir Jack's sword. It spun into the air in its helmet and splashed into the river below.

The headless body sat on the horse, still gripping its huge black sword.

After a moment of stunned horror, Sir Jack's men cheered. Sir Jack pulled off his helmet and rode back to them. Then he heard the sound of hooves behind him.

Sir Jack turned and saw the headless Black Knight ride towards him. Now the Black Knight's sword was raised.

"Prepare to die!" the Black Knight boomed.

Sir Jack did not stop to wonder how a man with no head could speak. Or ride a horse. Or raise a sword. He did not stop to wonder because he knew that the Black Knight was no mortal man.

He was a devil. No lucky charm could save Sir Jack now.

"Retreat! Flee!" Sir Jack wailed in terror. He dug his spurs into his horse's sides and galloped past his men. They too turned and fled.

Chapter 8
Cabbage

As soon as the last of Sir Jack de Zack's men disappeared from view, the sound of laughter filled Stonebridge Crossing.

Green Men dropped from their hiding places in the trees like ripe and rather brown fruit.

Physic the monk was too plump to climb trees and so he had hidden under straw in an old cart. He sat up and spat some straw from his mouth.

Big Jim had been hiding in the river under the bridge. He waded out of the water and helped Physic out of the cart.

Then they all gathered around the headless Black Knight, still on top of his huge horse. Big Jim banged on his tummy. "Are you all right in there, Squat?" he asked.

"I will be if you stop banging!" Squat said. "You are giving me a sore head." His voice sounded loud and deep as it boomed inside the armour.

The Green Men roared with laughter.

Friendly fished the Black Knight's helmet out of the river. It had a head in it all right. A head of cabbage!

The others helped Squat off the horse and out of the armour he only half filled.

Perhaps this picture will explain it best.

When Squat's feet were back on solid ground, Big Jim handed him the Black Knight's sword. Not that there ever was a real Black Knight, of course, just a large suit of armour with a very small man and a cabbage inside.

Squat took the sword and waved it above his head. The Green Men cheered. It was just a piece of wood, cut into a sword shape and painted black. There was no way Squat would have been able to lift his arm in the heavy armour and a heavy metal sword as well.

"No man has ever faced Sir Jack de Zack in combat and lived to tell the tale!" Friendly said.

"You didn't just live to tell the tale – you made him flee for his life!" said Robyn-in-the-Hat. She seemed to have appeared out of nowhere.

That night there was singing and drinking and laughter around the outlaws' campfire in Gressingham Forest. The Green Men all raised their cups to their new hero, the Black Knight of Gressingham.

58

But what of Sir Jack de Zack? He jumped on a boat back to France, gave all his gold to the poor, and he tried to be a good man for the rest of his days.

And what of Marshal Guppy? Well, he was furious. Which should come as no surprise. (He did a lot more SHOUTING.)

And what does this tale teach us? That good always wins over evil? Not always. But it does show us that some fights can be won with brains, even if you have a cabbage for a head.

Our books are tested
for children and young people by
children and young people.

Thanks to everyone who consulted on
a manuscript for their time and effort in
helping us to make our books better
for our readers.

Find out what happens next ...

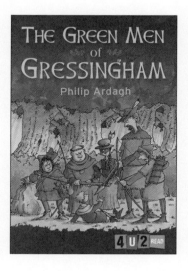

The Green Men are outlaws, living in a forest.
Now they have taken Tom prisoner!

What do they want from him?

Who is their secret leader, Robyn-in-the-Hat?

And whose side should Tom be on?

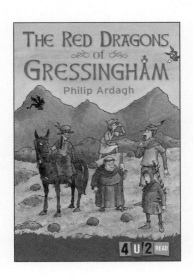

The Green Men used to be outlaws. Evil Marshal Guppy hated them. They lived in the forest and did brave deeds.

Now the Green Men are inlaws. Lord Dashwood really likes them. They live in the forest and do ... not very much.

The Green Men are *bored*.

They need some *fun*.

They need a *quest*.

www.barringtonstoke.co.uk

More *4u2read* titles ...

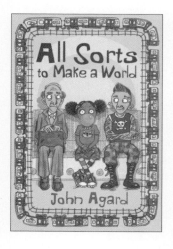

All Sorts to Make a World

JOHN AGARD

Shona's day has been packed with characters. First there was 3.2-million-year-old Lucy in the Natural History Museum, and then Pinstripe Man, Kindle Woman, Doctor Bananas and the iPod Twins.

Now Shona and her dad are on a Tube train that's stuck in a tunnel and everyone around them is going ... bananas!

Gnomes, Gnomes, Gnomes

ANNE FINE

Sam's obsessed. Any time he gets his hands on some clay, he makes gnomes. But Sam doesn't like to have gnomes in his room. So they live out in the shed. But when Sam's mum needs that space, the gnomes will have to go. So Sam plans a send-off that turns into a night the family will never forget!

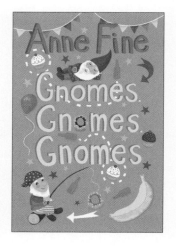

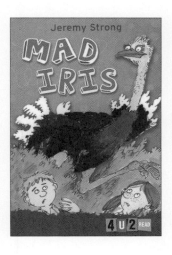

Mad Iris
JEREMY STRONG

Ross has a new pet – Mad Iris the ostrich! And she's got loose in the school!

Things are about to get really crazy...

Hostage
MALORIE BLACKMAN

"I'll make sure your dad never sees you again!"

Blindfolded. Alone. Angela has no idea where she is or what will happen next. The only thing she knows is she's been kidnapped. Is she brave enough to escape?

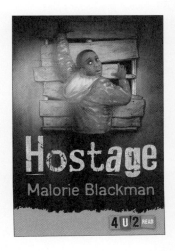

www.barringtonstoke.co.uk